Contents

A Note About This Story

This is an adventure story that takes place in Thailand in South-east Asia. To the south of Thailand is the beautiful blue water of the Gulf of Thailand.

Some of the people in this story live and work on boats. These pictures will help you.

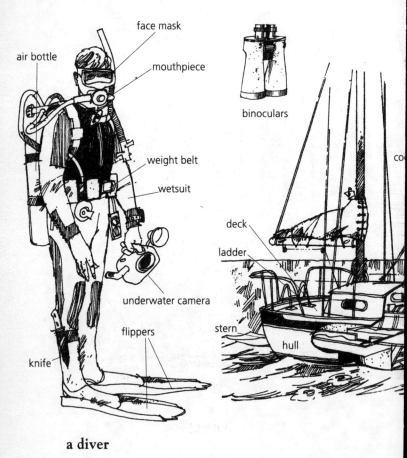

face mask
air bottle
mouthpiece
binoculars
weight belt
wetsuit
deck
ladder
underwater camera
stern
flippers
hull
knife

a diver

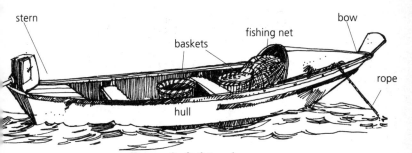

Daeng's fishing boat

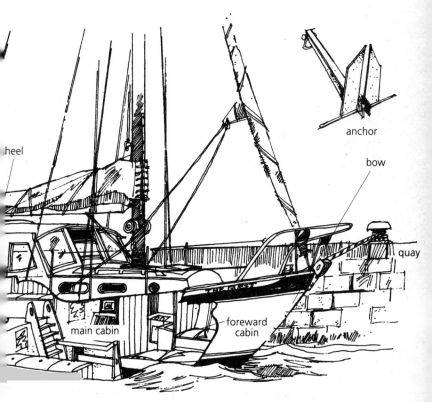

The Quest

The Places in This Story

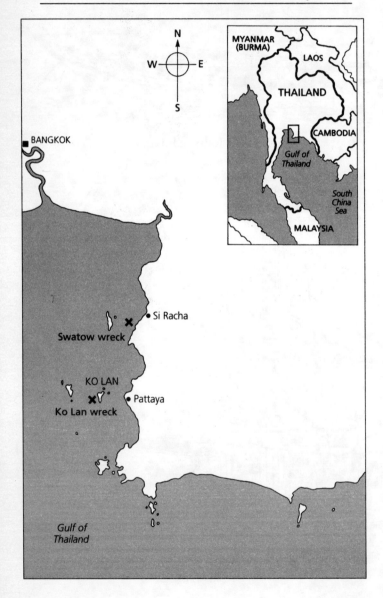

The People in This Story

Lek

Daeng

Mark Blackburn

John Morgan

The Collector

1

Daeng Finds the Plate

Daeng was worried. He looked up at the sky. It was clear and blue. He looked round him at the calm sea. There was no wind and the monsoon rains had not come yet. The monsoon would come soon. During the monsoon, there would be rain all day, every day, for weeks and weeks.

But today it was perfect weather for fishing. Daeng turned his eyes from the sky and looked at his boat. It was a good little fishing boat. He listened to the noise of the engine. Everything was all right. Why was he worried?

Daeng looked at the boy who was sitting quietly in the bottom of the boat. The boy was mending some fishing nets. Lek was a good boy. He helped Daeng a lot. Lek was clever and he learnt fast.

'What is wrong?' Daeng said to himself. He looked at the sky again. 'I have been a fisherman here in Si Racha for many years. But I have never been frightened before. And I don't understand why I am frightened. There is no reason for my fear.'

When he had no money for food, Daeng often went fishing in bad weather. He sailed his boat when the waves in the rough sea were huge. And he had never been frightened. Today the sea was calm, but he was frightened.

'We'll look for fish close to Si Racha today,' Daeng said to the boy. Lek looked up. He was surprised.

'But the weather is good,' said Lek. 'There is no wind.

Why don't you go further away from Si Racha? There are more fish away from land.'

'We'll stay here!' Daeng replied.

The boy said nothing. There was something wrong with Daeng today. Perhaps Daeng was worrying about his money problems. Daeng had bought the boat three months ago. It was very expensive.

Lek stood up and picked up the fishing net slowly.

———

Daeng stopped the boat and looked at the water. There were no rocks here. There was no danger. But he could not forget the words of the fortune-teller yesterday.

'Be careful at sea,' the fortune-teller had told him. 'There is death in the sea.'

What did the fortune-teller mean? Who was going to die? How were they going to die? What was going to kill them? A storm? Was Daeng's boat going to sink?

———

'OK! The fishing net is in the water now!' Lek shouted to Daeng.

The boat moved slowly forwards over the blue water.

Lek turned round and looked at Daeng. Daeng was worried.

'What is it?' asked Lek. 'Is everything OK?'

'I don't feel well,' Daeng said. 'We'll go back when we've pulled in the net. I'll be OK tomorrow.'

Suddenly the boat stopped moving.

Daeng leant over the side of the boat. He looked down into the water.

'The fishing net has caught on something!' he said.

Daeng went to the other side of the boat and looked into the water. 'I can't see anything,' he said.

'Are there any rocks here?' asked Lek.

Daeng shook his head. 'No, there aren't any rocks here.'

'What is it, then?' said Lek.

'I don't know, but we've got to pull the net into the boat again!' Daeng was worried.

Lek looked at him. Something was wrong. Now Lek began to worry too. There were monsters in the sea – huge monsters that ate people. Was the fishing net caught on a monster? Lek put a hand in his pocket and touched his knife.

'We must go backwards,' said Daeng. 'Then you can pull the net into the boat.'

Very slowly, Daeng reversed the boat. 'Can you pull the net in now?' he asked Lek.

Lek pulled the fishing net as hard as he could. But the fishing net still did not move. 'No!' Lek replied.

'Pull again!' Daeng told Lek.

Suddenly Lek shouted, 'Yes! It's coming!'

Daeng went quickly to the side of the boat and helped the boy. They started to pull the net into the boat.

'There are fish in the net!' Lek shouted. 'Look!'

Daeng looked into the net. He saw many silver fish there. But there was something else in the net. It was blue and white, and it was shining.

'What is that?' asked Daeng.

They pulled and pulled. At last, the fishing net lay in

the bottom of the boat. Lek stepped forward and opened the net. He picked up the blue and white thing. It was a plate.

Lek started to laugh.

'We've caught a plate! An old plate. Shall I throw it back into the sea?' he asked Daeng.

'No, no, wait a minute!' said Daeng. 'Give it to me.'

Daeng looked at the plate carefully.

'I saw a picture of a plate like this in a newspaper,' he said. 'The plate was very old. It was worth a lot of money.'

'But how did it get into our net?' asked Lek.

Daeng put the plate down and began to put the fish into baskets. When he had finished, he spoke to Lek.

'Perhaps there is a wreck down there.'

'A what?' asked the boy.

'A wreck – you know, a ship which sank a long time ago,' explained Daeng. 'There are lots of wrecks of old ships in the Gulf of Thailand. Perhaps that is why the net got caught. It was caught on a ship at the bottom of the sea. And this plate came from the ship.'

Daeng looked at the plate again.

'*Farang* – foreigners from America or Europe – often come to look for these wrecks,' he said. 'They go diving under the water to find things in the wrecks.'

Lek looked at the plate.

'Will you sell the plate?' he asked Daeng. 'Will you get a lot of money for it?'

'Perhaps if I sell it to a *farang*,' Daeng replied.

'We saw a *farang* this morning. Why don't you take the plate to him?' asked Lek. 'That *farang* is interested in wrecks.'

'That's a good idea. Yes. I'll take the plate to the *farang*. Perhaps he will buy it from me.'

Daeng wrapped the blue and white plate carefully in a piece of cloth. Then he turned the boat towards land. He was not excited. He was cold and afraid.

The boat moved quickly towards Si Racha. Daeng wanted to get there as quickly as possible.

2

On Board *The Quest*

In the harbour at Si Racha, there was a big, white sailing boat called *The Quest*. A young man with dark hair was standing on the quay beside the boat. He was hot and tired. He put down his two large bags.

'Hello?' he shouted. 'Is anyone there?'

A man came up into the cockpit of the boat. He had blue eyes and long blond hair. His skin was sunburnt. He walked over to the side of the boat and smiled.

'Are you John Morgan?' he said. 'Hello. I'm Mark Blackburn. Welcome aboard *The Quest*.'

John Morgan picked up his bags and climbed into the boat. The two men shook hands.

'I'm very pleased to meet you,' said John. 'I've read the books that you've written about old shipwrecks.'

'Well, perhaps I can show you some interesting ship-wrecks,' said Mark Blackburn. 'Come on, I'll take you to your cabin now.'

'Thanks,' replied John.

Mark went down some narrow steps. John followed him. As they reached the bottom, Mark said, 'This is the main cabin. It's where I work.'

On the walls of the cabin there were many maps. More maps and drawings covered the large wooden table. There were narrow windows all the way round the cabin. John looked through the windows and saw the blue water of Si Racha harbour outside.

They went through the main cabin and into a smaller cabin.

'This is your cabin. It's small but it's comfortable,' Mark said.

'Thank you,' John replied. He put his bags on the bed and they returned to the main cabin.

'What are you doing here in Si Racha?' John asked.

'I've found a sixteenth century Chinese wreck,' Mark explained.

'Where is the wreck?' asked John.

'It's near Ko Lan,' replied Mark. 'Ko Lan is an island near Pattaya. The wreck is here.' He pointed to one of the maps on the cabin wall.

'The wreck is quite close to the shore!' said John.

'Yes, and unfortunately, the tourist boats also go there. There is a lot of coral west of Ko Lan – here, you see?' Mark showed John the place on the map. 'The coral is very pretty, and tourists go diving there to see the coral and the fish. Then they take things from the wreck.'

'So did you find anything in the wreck?' asked John.

'Yes. The tourists left a few pieces of Chinese porcelain – cups and plates,' laughed Mark.

'Chinese porcelain? Sounds interesting. Tell me more,' John said.

'Hundreds of years ago, the Chinese traded with the Thais a lot,' Mark explained. 'They sold porcelain and other goods in Thailand and other parts of South-east Asia. Many ships were shipwrecked near here. One day, I'll find a wreck before the tourists!'

'Is Ko Lan the oldest wreck you've found?' asked John.

'No, I've found older wrecks. But none of those wrecks were in Asia,' said Mark. 'I would really like to find a wreck of a thirteenth or fourteenth century Chinese ship. Marco Polo wrote about those ships.'

'Marco Polo? The Italian who travelled to China at the end of the thirteenth century?' asked John.

'That's right,' Mark replied. 'Marco Polo lived in China for many years. He wrote about huge Chinese ships which sailed from China to India. They were very, very big. They had crews of 300 men.' He smiled at John. 'I want to find one of these ships.'

'Perhaps you'll be lucky,' said John. 'Well, when do we

go to the Ko Lan wreck?'

'As soon as possible,' Mark replied. 'It's too late to sail now, but we can sail early tomorrow. We don't have a lot of time to look at the wreck. We only have a week or two before the monsoon begins. When it starts raining, we will have to stop work.'

The two men went back up into the cockpit. A small group of Thai men were standing near *The Quest*. They were talking excitedly and pointing at the boat. When they saw Mark and John, they stopped talking. One of the men walked towards the boat. There was a boy behind him. Mark smiled at them.

'Hello. My name is Mark. Can I help you?' he asked.

'My name is Daeng,' the man replied, 'and this is my boat boy, Lek. We have found something in the sea. A plate. Perhaps it is from a wreck. Do you know about these things?'

'Yes,' said Mark. 'Come onto the boat and show me.'

Daeng and Lek climbed on board *The Quest*. The group of men on the quay watched them. Daeng was holding something wrapped in cloth. He gave it to Mark. Mark took it gently and unwrapped it.

For a moment Mark said nothing. He looked at the plate. Then he said softly, 'Swatow porcelain!'

'What is that?' asked Daeng.

'It's the name of this kind of Chinese porcelain,' replied Mark. 'How did you find it?'

'We were fishing. The net caught on something. We pulled in the net. The plate was in the net.'

'Mark, do you know how old this plate is?' asked John.

Mark turned the plate over. 'Yes, look here!' he said. 'There is some Chinese writing on the bottom of the plate. It says, "Great Ming Wan Li Year". Wan Li was Emperor of China from 1573 to 1620. That's late sixteenth to early seventeenth century.'

Mark looked at Daeng. 'This plate is very old. Where exactly were you fishing?' he asked.

Daeng did not answer Mark's question. Instead, Daeng replied, 'You can buy it.'

'I don't want the plate,' said Mark. 'I want to know where you were fishing. Perhaps there is more porcelain there. Perhaps there is a wreck. Show me where you found this plate. I'll pay you 25 000 baht.'

'Buy the plate,' Daeng said again.

'But I can't buy the plate! And you can't sell the plate!' replied Mark. 'This plate doesn't belong to you – it belongs to the Kingdom of Thailand. You must take the plate to the National Museum in Bangkok.'

Daeng picked up the plate. He began to walk away. The silent boy followed him.

'Wait,' Mark said. 'I can't buy the plate. Nobody can buy the plate. But show me where you found it. I'll pay you a lot of money. I'll pay you 50 000 baht.'

Daeng replied slowly. 'Fifty thousand baht?'

Mark nodded his head. 'Yes,' he said.

Daeng thought for a moment. 'OK, 50 000.'

'Good. Shall we meet tomorrow morning?'

'All right. My boat is with all the other fishing boats over there.' Daeng pointed to some Thai fishing boats not far from *The Quest*. 'Can you see the blue boat? That is my boat. We'll meet you at my boat at five-thirty.'

Mark and John watched the fisherman and the boy walk away. Then John spoke.

'Has anyone found Swatow porcelain in the Gulf of Thailand before?'

'No,' said Mark.

'So perhaps there is a new wreck here. Perhaps there is a lot of Chinese porcelain inside the hull,' said John.

Mark looked at him. 'It's possible,' he said. 'But why was that fisherman so frightened?'

3

A Sudden Death

'John! Wake up, it's five o'clock!' said Mark. 'Here's some coffee. Did you sleep well?'

'OK, thanks,' replied John sleepily.

John took the coffee and drank it quickly. It was dark outside.

'Will Daeng come?' John asked as he put on his clothes.

'I hope so,' Mark said. 'I want to find that wreck. I offered him a lot of money.' Mark looked at his watch.

'Let's go,' he said.

John and Mark climbed off *The Quest* and walked along the quayside. It was early and cool. There were still a few stars in the sky. But there were quite a lot of people on the streets. Some people were carrying baskets to the boats beside the water. Other people were riding bicycles to work. Shopkeepers were opening up their shops.

Mark and John walked quickly towards the small fishing boats. As they arrived at the boats, the first light of the sun appeared over the town. The stars disappeared. There was no wind and the sea was calm. Some fishermen were already in their boats. They were mending their nets. They were going fishing.

Mark and John walked to Daeng's boat. It was new and it was very tidy. There were nets and baskets along the sides of the boat. Everything was ready for fishing. But there was nobody on board.

'Hello? Daeng?' shouted Mark.

There was no reply. Some of the fishermen on the other boats turned their heads. They looked at the two *farang*.

'Well, he's not here yet, so we'll have to wait,' said John.

Mark and John sat down beside the boat. For a while, they enjoyed watching the fishermen. The sun rose in the sky. It got warmer.

Mark looked at his watch and got up.

'Where is Daeng?' he said. 'It's six o'clock.'

'Have you seen Daeng?' Mark asked the other fishermen. Nobody had seen Daeng.

'Perhaps he went to buy something for the boat,' said John. 'Perhaps he left a note in the boat. Why don't we look?'

The two men jumped down into the boat. They searched the boat carefully.

'There are no messages here,' said Mark. 'Look, we've been here for almost an hour. I don't think Daeng is going to come. Let's go. We've got work to do.'

By now, most of the fishing boats had left and the sun was quite high in the sky. Mark and John climbed out of Daeng's boat.

John looked down at Daeng's boat for the last time. Suddenly he stopped and went back to the edge of the quay.

'There's something in the water,' John said. He pointed down at the sea.

'What is it?' asked Mark.

'I don't know,' replied John. 'But I can see something shining there.'

Mark walked back and stood beside John.

'That's strange,' Mark said.

They got back into the boat and looked over the side.

'Hold my legs,' said Mark. 'I'll lean over the side.'

Slowly Mark leant over the side of the boat. Now he could see the thing in the water.

'Pull me up! Pull me up!' Mark shouted suddenly.

'What's the matter? What did you see? What was shining down there?' asked John.

Mark sat down suddenly in the boat.

'It's – it's a watch,' said Mark. 'The sun is shining on the glass of a watch.'

'A watch?' repeated John. 'What's frightening about a watch?'

'The watch is on Daeng's hand. Daeng is down there,' said Mark. 'He has been down there all this time.'

Mark's face became pale. He was frightened.

'I'll call the police,' said John.

4

Lek is in Danger

Mark and John were in the police station for a long time. The police officers asked them a lot of questions.

'Did you know the dead man?' they asked Mark and John. 'How long have you known him? What are you doing in Si Racha? Why did the dead man come to your boat? What did he tell you? Why were you waiting by his boat?'

At last, the police allowed Mark and John to leave the police station. The two men walked slowly back to *The Quest*. They did not speak.

Mark and John had not eaten all day. They were very tired. It was now two o'clock in the afternoon and the sun was high in the sky. It was very hot.

Mark and John climbed on board *The Quest*. Mark went to the fridge and took out a couple of bottles of juice. Then he opened a cupboard and found a packet of peanuts. He brought the juice and peanuts to John.

'Perhaps Daeng had an accident?' John asked.

'The police think that he had an accident,' Mark said. 'But I don't agree. Daeng was a fisherman. He could swim very well.'

'So Daeng was murdered?' asked John.

Mark nodded his head very slowly. 'Yes,' he said.

John put down his juice. 'But sometimes people fall into the water,' he said. 'Perhaps Daeng hit his head when he fell into the water. Sometimes there are accidents.'

'Yes. That's why it was such a good way to kill Daeng,' replied Mark.

'But why did somebody want to kill him?' asked John.

Mark got up and went to the fridge. He took out two more bottles of juice.

'Someone killed Daeng to stop him talking,' Mark said. 'Someone doesn't want us to know where the wreck is. Someone wants to find the wreck himself. A lot of people saw Daeng with the Swatow plate yesterday. Perhaps one of them killed Daeng.'

'So the murderer knew about the plate?' asked John. 'And the murderer knew about our meeting with Daeng?'

'In a small place like Si Racha, news travels fast,' replied Mark. 'The murderer wants to find the wreck himself.'

The two men sat silently for a while. They drank their juice.

At last John said, 'Perhaps Daeng told the murderer where he found the plate.'

'Yes,' said Mark. 'Perhaps the murderer made Daeng tell him where the wreck is. Then he killed Daeng.'

'Where do you think that the wreck is?' asked John.

'It could be anywhere,' Mark replied. 'It could be miles away from Si Racha.'

'Did the murderer take the Swatow plate?' asked John. 'When we searched Daeng's boat, I didn't see the plate.'

'Perhaps the murderer took it,' said Mark. 'Perhaps Daeng took it home. Perhaps Daeng sold the plate to a tourist.'

Mark and John looked across the water. The afternoon was very hot and still. A group of boys were laughing. They were playing in the water.

'But what about the boy?' John said suddenly.

'What boy?' asked Mark.

'Daeng's boat boy,' said John. 'The boy called Lek. The boy usually went fishing with Daeng. He was with Daeng yesterday. The boy knows where they found the plate.'

'Yes, you're right,' said Mark. He stood up quickly. 'But we have to find the boy before the murderer finds him. We have to find Lek.'

5

Lek Finds a Safe Place

Suddenly Lek heard a noise. He hid behind a wall. Was someone coming?

Lek listened for several minutes. Everything was quiet again. Perhaps there was nobody there. Perhaps it was safe to go home. Lek was very tired. Another minute passed and he heard nothing more.

The boat boy was hungry and thirsty and he was very frightened. It was not safe to go home. It was not safe to go anywhere in the town. But where could he go? How could he get help?

What was that noise? Lek looked round the corner of the wall. A dog was running across the street. There was no other sound, and no other movement. Everything was dark and quiet – except one boat. The lights of the boat shone in the darkness. Lek looked at the boat. It was a big, white sailing boat. It was the *farang*'s boat – *The Quest*.

Lek looked around him. There was nobody in the street. He looked at the windows of the houses beside the water. Nobody was watching. Quietly, Lek crossed the street and ran along the quay. He climbed onto *The Quest*.

———

Mark was standing in the main cabin. He was tired. Mark and John had searched all afternoon and all evening for the boy, Lek. But they had not found him.

'Let's go to sleep,' he said. 'We'll go to the Ko Lan

wreck tomorrow morning.'

John did not move. He was worried.

'We've been to Lek's home. We've been all along the quay. We've talked to the other fishermen. We've been to the market and we've talked to other boys. But nobody has seen him. He's disappeared!'

Suddenly they heard a soft sound.

'Ssh! What's that?' John said.

Mark ran up the steps quickly.

'There's someone on deck!' he said.

'Lek! What are you doing here?' whispered Mark to the boy. 'Where have you been? We've looked for you everywhere!'

Mark pulled Lek's arm. 'Come down into the cabin!' he told him.

Lek climbed down the steps into the main cabin. He was frightened and hungry. He did not know what to say. Both the foreigners were asking questions at the same time. He could not understand what they were saying.

Mark boiled some water and made some tea for the boy. 'Sit down,' he told him. 'Drink this.'

Lek drank the tea. Then John gave Lek a piece of chocolate. Lek ate it quickly.

'Are you feeling better now?' asked Mark.

'Yes, thank you,' Lek replied.

'OK, tell us what happened,' said John.

'There were two men,' explained Lek. 'They were *farang*. They came to Daeng's boat. They knew about the plate.'

'But why didn't you tell the police?' asked John.
Lek did not reply.

'Listen,' said Mark. 'Perhaps those men killed Daeng.
Perhaps they will try to kill you, too. You have to tell us
everything.'

'Yes.' Lek looked at Mark. He began to speak slowly.

'After Daeng spoke to you, he went home,' said Lek. 'But I stayed on the quay with some friends. Two men came. These men had heard about the plate. They asked me about the plate. I was stupid. I thought to myself, "These men will also give us money. Perhaps they will give us more money than the blond *farang*." So I told the men about our meeting at Daeng's boat. I told them where Daeng's boat was. I told them to come before five-thirty!'

Lek stood up. He covered his face with his hands. He was crying.

'It's my fault! I told the men about the plate! They were bad men, but I didn't know. And now Daeng is dead! Those men killed Daeng! It's my fault!' said Lek.

'Lek, what else do you know? Were you on Daeng's boat when the two men came?' asked John gently.

Lek was shaking. 'Yes. Last night I slept on the boat. The bad men did not see me when they arrived. I was sleeping under some blankets.'

'What did you see?' asked Mark.

'When I woke up, I saw the men,' Lek replied. 'They were hitting Daeng. Next, they threw him into the water. Then they took the plate and they ran away. And I ran away too. I could not tell anyone about this. But you are good people. You are not like those men. You found Daeng. You went to the police.'

Lek's face was wet with tears.

'These men – the murderers – they will search for me,' Lek went on. 'And they will kill me, too!'

Mark put his hand on the boy's arm.

'The men who killed Daeng won't find you,' he said. 'You can stay here on *The Quest*. The killers won't look for you here. You're safe with us. Don't worry.'

Mark quickly found blankets and prepared a bed for Lek. In five minutes, the boy was asleep.

Mark watched Lek. The boy was crying in his sleep. Then Mark returned to the main cabin.

'Is Lek safe?' John asked Mark quietly. 'Won't the killers look for him here?'

'No, Lek isn't safe, and we aren't safe either,' said Mark. 'Those men will come and look for Lek here. So we must go.'

'Leave now? Sail in the dark?' asked John.

'Yes,' replied Mark. 'We can't wait for the morning. We must go now. We'll start looking for the Swatow wreck very early, when it's light. Let's go.'

6

The Search for the Swatow Wreck

'We found the plate near here!' shouted Lek.

The Quest was sailing slowly along the coast. It was a wonderful morning. The wind was blowing gently into the sails of the boat. The sun was shining on the water. Mark was in *The Quest*'s cockpit. He was holding the wheel and steering the boat. John was standing on the deck. He was looking at the land in the distance.

'Are you sure?' Mark asked the boy. 'Were you so close to the land?'

'Yes. Two days ago we were very close to the land,' said Lek.

'OK, we'll stop here,' said Mark. 'Drop the anchor into the water.'

Lek and John threw the heavy anchor into the water. A few seconds later, *The Quest* stopped moving. Mark and John took down the boat's sails.

Lek helped Mark and John get ready for their first dive under the water. Mark and John put on their wetsuits and weight belts. Next, Lek helped the men to put heavy metal bottles on their backs.

'We can stay under the water for quite a long time with these bottles of air,' explained Mark. 'We breathe air through a mouthpiece, here.' Mark showed the mouthpiece to Lek.

Then Mark and John put on long yellow flippers. The flippers were going to help them swim quickly and easily through the water.

Lek passed Mark and John their face masks. Mark and John put the masks on. Then they put the mouthpieces in their mouths. They were ready. It was time to go.

Mark and John moved to the stern of the boat. Then they jumped into the cool blue water.

When he came to the surface, Mark looked at his watch. Then he put his head under the water. He could not see the sea-bed. What was at the bottom of the sea?

They jumped into the cool blue water.

Was there a wreck here at all?

Mark started to swim down to the sea-bed. It was flat and sandy.

When Mark reached the bottom he turned round. John was just behind him.

John made a sign with his hand to tell Mark, 'Everything is OK!' Then they looked slowly around them. They could not see the wooden hull of a ship. They could not see any broken cups or plates lying on the sea-bed.

Mark and John searched for forty minutes, but they did not find anything. Then Mark looked at his diver's watch. He showed John the time on his watch. Mark pointed up with his thumb. They had to return to The Quest.

Mark and John swam up slowly. Finally, their heads were above the water. They pulled off their face masks and flippers. Then they climbed into the boat.

Lek helped them to take off their air bottles. 'Did you find anything?' he asked.

Mark shook his head. He wiped the sea water from his eyes. 'No,' he said. 'I've never found a wreck on the first dive. Sometimes I have to search for months.'

Lek was worried. 'But the monsoon!' he said. 'The big rains are coming. The weather will be very bad in a couple of weeks, perhaps sooner.'

'Yes, I know,' said Mark. 'But we've still got a few days. If the Swatow wreck is here, we'll find it.'

———

A few days passed, but they did not find the wreck. Mark

and John went diving every day. Every day, they searched another part of the sea-bed.

On the third evening, Mark and John were sitting in the cockpit of *The Quest*. They were drinking coffee. Lek was sleeping in the small cabin below. It was a wonderful, warm night and the stars shone brightly.

'Do you think Lek has made a mistake? Is this the wrong place?' asked John.

Mark drank his coffee slowly.

'Perhaps,' he replied. 'But we'll search for a couple more days. Perhaps we'll be lucky.'

———

The next day, the wind started blowing. The sea was no longer calm. High up in the sky there were clouds. *The Quest* moved up and down on the sea.

Lek pointed to the clouds. He was worried.

'The monsoon is coming!' he said.

'We must work quickly,' said Mark. 'Let's go.'

Mark and John got ready for diving and jumped into the sea. It was difficult to see under the water. The water was full of sand. The movement of the sea was pulling the sand up from the sea-bed.

Mark and John swam down to the sea-bed. Then John stopped and pointed ahead of them. At first, Mark could not see anything. Then, suddenly, he saw something lying on the sea-bed.

Mark swam closer. He saw some pieces of wood in the sand. They were pieces of wooden hull! It was the wreck. They had found the Swatow wreck!

Mark and John swam round the hull once. They looked at it carefully. Then they swam back up to *The Quest*.

Lek was waiting for them on *The Quest*. Mark and John took off their flippers and climbed onto the boat.

'We've found the wreck!' said John.

'Did you see any more porcelain?' asked Lek.

'No,' John answered him. 'The hull is under a lot of sand. We need to move some of the sand away. Then we can see if there is any more porcelain.'

Suddenly it began to rain hard. The wind blew more strongly. The waves in the sea got bigger. Mark looked up at the sky. The sun was hidden by clouds.

'We haven't got much time,' Mark said. 'We must go back down again! John, take the torch and the underwater camera. And take a net for the porcelain. Lek, there are some full air bottles over there. Can you see them? Pass them to us! Quickly! Let's go! Let's go!'

Mark and John jumped back into the water.

_____

On the coast, far away from Mark's boat, a man was sitting in a car. The car was hidden behind some trees at the edge of the water.

The man was watching *The Quest*. He was looking through powerful binoculars. He had been sitting in the car all day and watching *The Quest*.

The man picked up the mobile phone that was on the seat beside him. He dialled a number. A voice answered immediately.

'They've found the wreck,' the man said.

7

Treasure

For two days, Mark and John worked on the wreck. First, they took a lot of photographs of the wooden hull. Then they began to move the sand away from the hull.

Moving the sand was a very slow and tiring job. The weather was bad and it was dark under the water. The two men could not see very well.

When Mark and John swam up to the surface after a dive, it was difficult to get back onto the boat. The sea was very rough. The waves lifted the boat up. Then the boat fell back down heavily.

———

Mark and John were getting ready to dive again late on the second afternoon.

'Please don't dive again. Let's go back to Si Racha!' shouted Lek. The noise of the wind was very loud. 'The wind is very strong. Look at the sea. The waves are going to get bigger – much bigger. It's not safe on the water. We must go now.'

Mark looked at the sea and then he looked up at the sky. He did not want to leave the wreck. He wanted to know what was inside the hull. They had cleared most of the sand away from the deck.

'Lek is right,' said John. 'It is too dangerous. Mark, we know where the wreck is now. We can come back after the monsoon is over.'

'Let's dive once more. Perhaps this last dive will be the lucky one,' said Mark.

Lek and John looked at Mark.

'One more dive,' Mark repeated. 'Then we'll return to Si Racha.'

There was a silence.

'OK,' said John at last. He put on his face mask and picked up the net. Then the two men jumped into the water.

Lek watched them go. He was worried. He knew the danger of the monsoon. He wanted to get back to land as soon as possible. They would be safer on land than out on the sea. He was more frightened of the storm than of Daeng's murderers.

Mark and John reached the wreck. John held the torch. Mark cleared away the sand.

Suddenly Mark stopped and took the torch. He was pointing at something. It was a hole in the wooden hull. The hole was big enough for them to swim through. Now they could get inside!

Carefully, they swam through the hole. Mark shone the light of the torch ahead of them. It was very dark inside. Then suddenly, Mark saw something in the sand. It was a blue and white plate!

Mark looked round at John. He pointed at the plate. Then he began to dig under the sand. He found more beautiful Chinese porcelain plates. Mark passed the plates to John. John put the plates in the net.

Mark worked hard. They had to leave soon. He found

It was a blue and white plate!

more pieces of porcelain, a bowl, then a beautiful vase, then a large red plate. Then Mark dug up more bowls and some cups. The net became very heavy.

After a few minutes, John touched Mark's shoulder. He pointed to his watch. Mark nodded his head. It was time to go back to the boat.

Mark and John picked up the net together. They began to swim slowly back up to the boat.

When they were near the surface, Mark touched John's arm and pointed. John turned his head and looked up. Next to the hull of *The Quest*, he could see the hull of another boat. The two men looked at each other.

Mark and John reached the surface quickly. They looked at the boat beside *The Quest*. The second boat was a new and expensive motor boat. Mark and John could not see anybody on board the motor boat. They could not see Lek, either.

'Lek!' Mark shouted.

There was no reply.

'Here, John, you take the net,' said Mark. 'I'll climb on board *The Quest*. Then I can pull up the net.'

A big wave lifted *The Quest*. Mark waited. The boat dropped down into the water. Mark grabbed the ladder and climbed up. Then he understood why Lek had not answered his shout.

Lek was lying on the deck of *The Quest*. He had a cloth tied over his mouth and his hands were tied behind his back.

8

The Collector

A man was sitting in the cockpit of *The Quest*. He was a small man, about fifty years old. He had dark hair and a thin, clever face. He was wearing sunglasses.

The Quest was moving up and down on the rough sea, but the man was comfortable and relaxed. There were two men beside him. The men were tall and strong. They were holding guns. The guns were pointing at Mark. The small man stood up when he saw Mark.

'Welcome aboard, Mr Blackburn,' said the small man.

'Who are you?' asked Mark. 'What do you want? What are you doing on my boat? Untie the boy!'

'I will not tell you my name, Mr Blackburn,' replied the small man. 'However, some people call me the Collector. But please, come over here. And tell your friend to join us. My assistants will help him to bring the net on board. We don't want to lose any of that beautiful porcelain.'

The Collector spoke to one of his men. The man had a scar on his face. He went to the stern of the boat. The other man pointed his gun at Mark.

'Do what the man says, John!' shouted Mark. 'Give him the net and then come up!'

The man with the scar threw down a rope. John tied the rope to the net. The man lifted it carefully onto the deck. Then John climbed on board *The Quest*.

'Now stand next to your friend,' the Collector told John.

'Welcome aboard, Mr Blackburn.'

'What's happening? Who are you?' asked John.

The Collector did not reply. He took off his sunglasses and sat down beside the net.

'Well, well, you have been very busy,' he said. 'What have we got here?'

The Collector picked up some blue and white porcelain plates. He looked at them carefully.

'Swatow porcelain,' he said. 'Nice. Very nice. Very valuable.'

The Collector put the plates down gently and picked up a bowl. On the bowl there was a beautiful picture of a moon and a bird.

'Now, look at this!' said the Collector. 'What a lovely bowl.' He looked at the bowl carefully. 'Yes, it's Wan Li. It's definitely Wan Li,' he said. 'This ship must have sunk between 1573 and 1620. Do you agree, Mr Blackburn?'

Mark was very angry. 'Tell your men to put their guns down. And untie Lek.'

The Collector did not listen to him. He was looking at four beautiful plates. He was smiling.

'Now, here are some very pretty plates,' the Collector said softly. 'Good. Very good. These are worth a lot of money.'

'But they're not for sale,' said Mark.

The Collector looked at Mark and smiled. 'People always want to buy beautiful old things, Mr Blackburn,' he said. 'People will pay a lot of money for antiques. I know people in New York, London, Zurich, Hong Kong and Amsterdam who will want to buy this porcelain.'

Then the Collector picked up something small and smooth. 'Well, well ... what is this?' he asked Mark.

Mark looked at the object.

'You won't get any money for that. It's a duck egg,' said Mark. 'There are several jars of eggs in the wreck. They were food for the sailors.'

'How interesting,' said the Collector. He looked at Mark.

'Mr Blackburn, I like you,' he told Mark. 'I have read your books. They are most interesting. You and I have the same interests. We like wrecks. We like beautiful old porcelain. Why don't we work together?'

'I don't work with murderers,' Mark replied. 'You killed Daeng.'

The Collector put on his sunglasses again.

'Yes. I'm sorry that the fisherman died. Unfortunately, he didn't want to tell my assistants about the wreck.' The Collector pointed towards the tall men beside him. 'These men help me with my work.'

Mark stepped forward.

'Get off my boat, and take your men with you,' he told the Collector.

'Of course, Mr Blackburn,' the Collector replied. He picked up the net and the porcelain. 'We must leave you now. The weather is getting worse. Goodbye, Mr Blackburn. It was a pleasure to meet you.'

The Collector said something to his two men. They turned and started to go back to their boat.

Suddenly a huge wave hit *The Quest*. Green sea water

poured over the boat. The wave knocked the men down.

Mark was the first to stand up again. The Collector and his men were still struggling in the water. Mark was behind the man with the scar. He reached down quickly and grabbed the man's gun.

'Mark, be careful! Look behind you!' shouted John.

John's shout came too late. The other gunman had got up quickly too. He lifted his gun and hit Mark on the back of the head.

9

The Quest in Trouble

John saw Mark fall beside Lek onto the deck of the boat. Quickly he put on his face mask. He moved to the side of the boat and jumped into the sea. Then he dived down under *The Quest*.

John thought quickly. The Collector and his men were on *The Quest*. Lek was tied up and Mark was hurt. He must do something, but what could he do?

'Perhaps I could swim to the coast and get help?' he thought. 'No – the sea is too rough. I couldn't swim that far. Perhaps I could climb on board the motor boat? Then I could start the engine and escape. But what about Mark and Lek? I can't leave them.'

John looked up at the hulls of the two boats above him. He was very cold, tired and frightened.

'I must do something,' John said to himself. But he could not think of anything to do.

He looked up at the hulls again. *The Quest* looked strange. It was very low in the water. What was happening? Was *The Quest* sinking?

'I must do something ...' John repeated to himself. But he was very cold and tired, and the movement of the water was making him feel sick. It was difficult to think clearly.

Suddenly, the motor boat's powerful engines started. A moment later, the motor boat moved away. Then there was only the hull of *The Quest*.

John lay quietly in the water. He was feeling very strange. He was not cold any more. Now the movement of the water made him very tired. He closed his eyes.

Suddenly, John felt a hard knock on his head. He opened his eyes and looked around. *The Quest* was very low in the water. He had hit his head on the hull.

He swam up through the water. At last, his face was above the water. He pulled out his mouthpiece and breathed the fresh air. He began to feel better. He looked at *The Quest*. The waves were pouring over the sides of the boat. *The Quest* was going to sink very soon.

John grabbed the ladder at the stern of *The Quest*. He pulled himself up into the cockpit.

'Mark! Lek!' he shouted as he took off his face mask. 'Are you OK?'

Mark rubbed his head. 'Yes,' he said. 'Quick! Untie Lek.'

John untied the ropes around Lek.

The Quest *looked strange. It was very low in the water.*

'Why are we sinking?' John asked Mark.

'Quick! The Collector's men opened the seacock!' shouted Mark, and he ran down into the main cabin. John followed him.

The main cabin was almost full of sea water. Books, cups and papers were floating in the water.

The seacock was a tap at the bottom of the boat. If it was opened, the boat filled with water.

At first, Mark and John could not reach the seacock. They tried again and again. At last they reached the seacock and turned it off.

Lek came down into the cabin with three life jackets. 'Here – put these on,' he said. John and Mark each put one on.

'The radio!' shouted Mark. 'We have to send a mayday message!'

The radio was on a high shelf in the main cabin. It was not yet under the water.

Mark quickly grabbed the radio.

'Mayday! Mayday! Mayday!' Mark shouted into the microphone. 'This is *The Quest*, *The Quest*. We are eight miles west of Si Racha. We are sinking! There are three people on board.' He repeated the radio message again and again.

'John, quickly – get the pump,' said Mark.

John began to pump the water out of the boat. Lek found a bucket. He began to throw the water out of the boat.

Mark waited for a reply to his radio message. No reply

'Mayday! Mayday! Mayday!'

came. Mark repeated his message. Again there was no reply.

'Nobody can hear us,' said Mark at last. 'There are no other boats near here.'

Mark found another bucket. He went to help John and Lek. But *The Quest* was still sinking. The sea was very rough now. Huge waves threw more and more sea water into *The Quest*.

No one said anything. Mark, John and Lek worked as quickly as they could. They continued to pump and to throw buckets of water out of the boat. Slowly, the water in the cabin started to go down.

'We're winning!' Mark shouted. 'The water is lower. Keep working!'

At last, the water only covered their feet. After an hour, the three of them rested. They were very, very tired.

It was dark now and the wind was blowing strongly. The waves crashed over the boat.

'We can't stay here all night,' said Mark. 'We must sail to the coast now.'

'But we can't see anything in the dark,' said John. 'Can't we wait until the storm has finished?'

'This isn't a storm!' shouted Lek. 'This is the monsoon. You can wait for a storm to finish. But monsoons go on for many days.'

10

Through the Monsoon

Mark sailed *The Quest* towards the coast. The speed of the boat was frightening.

'Mountains!' shouted John to Lek above the loud noise of the wind. 'These waves are like mountains!'

It was impossible to see the coast. The waves and the rain fell on the boat all the time.

John was terrified. But Mark was a very good sailor. Although the storm was very bad, *The Quest* was sailing through it. They were not very far from land and soon they would be in the harbour at Si Racha. John was tired, hungry and thirsty.

Suddenly there was a shout.

'Look! Behind us!'

The shout came from Lek. He was pointing behind the boat. John turned round. He saw a huge wave of dark water above their heads. The water was much higher than the boat. This enormous wave was about to fall on them.

'Hold on!' Mark screamed to John and Lek.

The water hit *The Quest*. It threw the men across the boat. Mark tried to get up. But then another huge wave came. *The Quest* almost rolled over.

'Hold on!' shouted Mark again.

John and Lek held on to the side of the boat. They were very frightened. 'If another wave hits us, we'll roll over,' said John.

'If another wave hits us, we'll roll over.'

Quickly, Mark got back to the steering wheel. He turned the wheel and *The Quest* turned round. Now the wind and waves were behind the boat again.

'Is everyone all right?' Mark shouted. John and Lek shouted, 'Yes!'

'We were going too fast,' Mark explained. 'We have to slow down!'

'Slow down? How can we slow down?' asked John.

'Get those two ropes over there,' Mark told John. He pointed to two long thick ropes. John picked them up.

'Now tie them together,' said Mark. 'Tie one end of the rope to the stern ladder. Then throw the other end into the sea.'

John tied the ropes together. He pulled them to the stern of the boat and tied one end to the boat. Then he threw the other end into the sea. When all the rope was in the water behind the boat, *The Quest* slowed down.

Suddenly, Lek shouted, 'Look!' He pointed in front of the boat.

Mark and John saw a bright red light in the sky in front of them.

'That's an emergency flare!' shouted Mark. 'Someone is in trouble!'

'The flare is quite near. What shall we do?' asked John.

'We must go and help,' Mark replied. 'There are no other boats near here.'

Mark steered *The Quest* towards the red light in the sky. For a few moments, the red light shone on the waves. Then the light went out, and everything was dark again.

For a while Mark, John and Lek saw nothing. Then another flare lit up the sky. This time the flare was above *The Quest*.

'We're very close!' shouted Mark.

As they got to the top of the next wave, they saw something in the water. It was the hull of a boat. The boat had rolled over in the water. Three people were holding on to the hull of the boat.

Mark steered *The Quest* closer to the hull. It was very difficult to see through the heavy rain. But then John saw something.

'It's the Collector and his men!' he shouted.

Lek looked at the men, then he grabbed Mark's arm.

'Those murderers killed Daeng!' Lek shouted. 'They tried to kill us! They're dangerous! Leave them!'

Mark began to steer *The Quest* past the motor boat. The Collector and his two men saw *The Quest*. They began to wave and to shout for help.

'Stop! Save us!' the Collector shouted.

'Help!' shouted one of the Collector's men.

'You can't leave us!' shouted the other man.

'No! No!' Lek shouted to Mark. 'Don't stop! Leave the murderers here!'

They began to wave and to shout for help.

11

The Collector Again

A few weeks later, Mark and John were sitting in the main cabin of *The Quest*. The two young men had just returned from the Swatow wreck. *The Quest* was tied up to the quay in Si Racha.

The monsoon was finished. The weather was sunny and the sea was calm. On the table in front of Mark and John were some objects from the Swatow wreck.

'What are those?' asked John, pointing to some small pieces of metal on the table.

'They're coins,' Mark replied. Then he picked up another small object. 'And this is a mirror. I found them inside the hull of the Swatow wreck.'

'Are they Chinese coins?' asked John.

'Yes,' said Mark. 'Many years ago Chinese shipbuilders put coins and a mirror inside the hulls of wooden ships. This brought the sailors good luck and good winds,' he explained. 'There are seven coins. The shipbuilders put the coins like this.'

John looked at the arrangement of coins. 'What does that mean?' he asked.

'It is the same shape as a group of stars in the night sky. We call that group of stars the Big Bear,' Mark said.

Mark put the mirror above the coins.

'The coins are the stars, and the mirror is the moon. Modern shipbuilders put this sign in new ships. But they

don't use coins. They use nails for the stars. And they use
a silver coin for the moon.'

John picked up the coins and looked at them.

'Good luck and good winds,' he said. 'The coins and
the mirror didn't help the Swatow ship!'

Mark laughed. 'No, they didn't.'

'What are you going to do now?' asked John. 'You've
finished your work here now. All the porcelain from the
Swatow wreck is safe in the National Museum.'

'Most of the porcelain is in the National Museum,' said
Mark. 'The porcelain that the Collector took from us is at
the bottom of the sea. He will never find it!'

'So are you going to look for another wreck now?'

Mark smiled. He looked through the window and out at
the sea.

'Yes, but where is that wreck?' he said. 'Where do I
look?'

Suddenly, Lek climbed down into the main cabin. He was worried. He was holding a newspaper.

'Mark! John! The Collector! He's free!'

'What does it say in the newspaper?' asked Mark.

Lek sat down on a chair and began to read.

'It says that the three men have been in prison for three months. But the police could not keep them in prison for killing Daeng. No one saw Daeng's murderer. Perhaps Daeng died in an accident.'

'Lek, you saw what happened. Why didn't you tell the police?' asked John. 'We took the men to the police station but you didn't come with us! Now the Collector is free!'

Lek was suddenly angry with John.

'It was too dangerous!' he shouted. 'The Collector is too powerful. I told you to leave him and his men in the sea! They murdered Daeng!'

'Lek! I couldn't leave the men to die in the storm,' said Mark.

Suddenly, there was a shout from outside the boat.

'Mr Blackburn!'

Mark got up and went up onto the deck.

'Yes?' he said.

A small boy was standing on the quay. He was holding something in his arms. It was big and it was wrapped in a piece of cloth.

'This is for you,' said the boy.

'What is it? Who is it from?' asked Mark.

'I don't know,' said the boy. 'A man gave it to me. He didn't say his name. He told me to give it to Mr Blackburn, on a boat called *The Quest*.'

'OK, thanks,' Mark said. He gave the boy some money.

Mark went back into the cabin and sat down.

'What is it?' asked John.

'It's something quite heavy,' Mark said.

Very slowly, he unwrapped it. Inside the cloth, there was a beautiful Chinese vase.

John spoke first.

'Wow!' he said. 'Is it older than the Swatow porcelain? Who sent it?'

'I don't know,' said Mark. 'Wait a minute—' Mark held the vase up.

'There is some Chinese writing on the bottom of the vase,' he said. 'This is a Yuan vase!'

'Yuan? What does that mean?' asked Lek.

'It was made when the Yuan emperors ruled China,' Mark explained. 'This vase is very, very old. It was made in about 1350.'

'Then it's much older than the Swatow plate!' said Lek.

John looked at the piece of cloth again. 'Look, Mark,' he said. 'Someone has drawn a picture on the cloth.'

'A picture? A picture of what?' asked Lek.

'I don't know,' said Mark. 'I don't understand.' He turned the cloth around and around.

John looked at the piece of cloth. 'It's not a picture. It's a map. See – this is China. And here's Korea —'

'Yes, of course!' said Mark. 'Look! That's the coast of Korea, not far from Shinan in China. But what's this? It looks like a cross. A cross in the sea, off Shinan.'

Inside the cloth there was a beautiful Chinese vase.

'Have any wrecks been found there?' asked John.

'No,' replied Mark slowly. 'No. Not yet!'

Mark put the beautiful vase down gently on the table.

'1350 ... a Yuan vase ... a map marked with a cross,' Mark said quietly.

He leant back on the seat and closed his eyes.

'A fourteenth century Chinese wreck, near the coast of Shinan,' Mark went on. 'In those days, Chinese people traded with many countries. Ships from China sailed many thousands of miles. They went to Korea and Japan, to the coast of Africa, to Zanzibar and Madagascar.'

'Mark, when we first met, you told me your dream,' said John. 'You wanted to find a thirteenth or fourteenth century wreck. A ship from the time of Marco Polo.'

'Who was Marco Polo?' asked Lek.

Mark opened his eyes and smiled. 'Tell him, John.'

'Marco Polo was born in Italy about seven hundred years ago. He travelled from Italy to China. His journeys took many years. Marco Polo wrote about his travels. He wrote about huge ships that sailed from China to India. These ships had crews of 300 men —'

John was looking at the vase. 'Wait a minute,' he said. 'There's something in it.' He pulled out a piece of paper.

'What is it?' asked Mark.

John looked closely at the paper.

'It's a message,' he replied. 'It says, "Good luck and good winds! Thanks, the Collector." '

Points for Understanding

1

1 Who is Daeng?
2 What does he do?
3 What did Daeng find in his fishing net?

2

1 What is Mark Blackburn's job?
2 Why is he in Thailand?
3 Why did Daeng show Mark the plate?

3

1 How long did Mark and John wait for Daeng?
2 Who did they meet in Daeng's boat?
3 Where was Daeng?

4

1 Why does Mark think that Daeng was murdered?
2 Who do Mark and John want to find?
3 Why do they want to find him?

5

1 Why did Lek go to *The Quest*?
2 What did Lek tell the two men on the quay?
3 Why is Lek frightened?

6

1 What did Mark and John find on their first dive?
2 Why is the good weather going to change?
3 What happened on shore when they found the wreck?

7

1 How did the bad weather make life difficult for Mark and John?
2 What did they find in the wreck?
3 What happened while they were under the water?

8

1 Who were the men on *The Quest*?
2 What did these men want?
3 What happened when the wave fell on the boat?

9

1 How did John escape?
2 What did the Collector's men do to *The Quest*?
3 How did John, Mark and Lek save *The Quest*?

10

1 What was the weather like?
2 Why did Mark turn back when he saw the flare?
3 Whose boat was in trouble?

11

1 What was in the cloth?
2 Who was it from?
3 Why are the map and the vase so important?

ELEMENTARY LEVEL

A Christmas Carol *by Charles Dickens*
Riders of the Purple Sage *by Zane Grey*
The Canterville Ghost and Other Stories *by Oscar Wilde*
Lady Portia's Revenge and Other Stories *by David Evans*
The Picture of Dorian Gray *by Oscar Wilde*
Treasure Island *by Robert Louis Stevenson*
Road to Nowhere *by John Milne*
The Black Cat *by John Milne*
The Red Pony *by John Steinbeck*
The Stranger *by Norman Whitney*
Tales of Horror *by Bram Stoker*
Frankenstein *by Mary Shelley*
Silver Blaze and Other Stories *by Sir Arthur Conan Doyle*
Tales of Ten Worlds *by Arthur C. Clarke*
The Boy Who Was Afraid *by Armstrong Sperry*
Room 13 and Other Stories *by M.R. James*
The Narrow Path *by Francis Selormey*
The Lord of Obama's Messenger and Other Stories
by Marguerite Siek
Why Ducks Sleep on One Leg and Other Stories *by Anne Ingram*
The Gift from the Gods and Other Stories *by Anne Ingram*
The Land of Morning Calm and Other Stories *by Anne Ingram*
Love Conquers Death and Other Stories *by Catherine Khoo and Marguerite Siek*
The Stone Lion and Other Stories *by Claire Breckon*
The Bride of Prince Mudan and Other Stories *by Celine C. Hu*

For further information on the full selection of Readers at all five levels in the series, please refer to the Heinemann ELT Readers catalogue.

Macmillan Heinemann English Language Teaching

A division of Macmillan Publishers Limited

Companies and representatives throughout the world

ISBN 0 435 27304 3

First published 1999

Editorial development by Phoenix Publishing Services
Illustrated by Trevor Ridley
Map on page 6 by John Gilkes
Typography by Adrian Hodgkins
Designed by Sue Vaudin
Cover by Paul Campion and Marketplace Design
Typeset in 11½/14½pt Goudy
Printed and bound in Spain by Mateu Cromo

99 00 01 02 10 9 8 7 6 5 4 3 2 1